WATCH ME

E.M. GAYLE

GYPSY INK BOOKS

Description:

Welcome to Purgatory! A club for every desire.

For as long as she could remember, Emerson wanted only one man. But he wanted nothing to do with her. Until she discovered his secret--in a sex club. With a mask and a plan she goes after him and ends up unearthing her own secret desires.

Rio wants what he can't have but isn't about to ruin his life over it. Now a new woman has caught his eye and he longs to discover why she hides.

As they get closer to the truth, the tension escalates and the forbidden becomes irresistible.

CHAPTER 1

"Em, are you really going to go through with this?" Katie yelled over the loud music pounding through the club.

"Of course I am. It's what I've been working up to for months now. Why would I back out now?"

"Oh, I don't know. Because maybe when you take off that mask and Rio gets one look at the real you, you'll be a dead woman."

Em looked at her friend's frightened expression, trying not to laugh. It had taken a long time getting to know the people here at Purgatory before she'd built up the nerve to tell anyone who she really was. Now she was tired of hiding, and ready to unveil her identity once and for all. She didn't want to think about the public humiliation Rio could put her through if he made a scene. She worried too much about him as it was.

"You know they don't allow masks at the private after-hours party. If I want to take the next step in my journey, and I do, then I have no choice but to reveal myself. Rio be damned." If the man wasn't already damned. She looked up at where he stood, watching one of the play stations. Master D's station, of course. She couldn't tell what he was doing tonight, but she knew it was one of the more hardcore stations they offered where they did things like violet wand or needle play.

From this vantage point, she stared at Rio's profile. Wavy dark hair, tanned skin from working outdoors with her brother, and all black leather—from the vest to the pants that hugged what she knew was the most perfect ass on the planet, to the black leather boots he wore on his feet.

Here in this environment, he made it impossible to read his body language. She found him guarded, more often than not with a stern expression. Some went so far as to refer to him as El Diablo, the devil himself.

"Em, last dance of the night and I have a slot center stage with no one to fill it. You want it?" Gabriel, the club manager, had sneaked up behind her while she ogled Rio for the umpteenth time that night. She tore her gaze away and turned to Gabe with a smile on her face.

"You want me?"

"Ahh, my dear, you have no idea. Everyone wants the elusive Em."

"I find that hard to believe."

"Why is that?"

She shrugged. She wouldn't get into her insecurities with Gabe. Here in the club things were different for her. She wasn't the sweet little Emerson whom no one ever spoke to.

No, here she was bold and wanton, and reveled in the attention of the many patrons who liked to watch her. Even Rio. He'd been cool about it, of course, never showing too much interest, but there'd been a few times where she'd caught his gaze as he watched her play. She'd thought the heat in his eyes matched the arousal coursing through her body at his perusal, but so far he'd been aloof, never approaching her.

"So, darlin', do you want to take the chains?"

She'd been eyeing that platform for a long time, wondering what it would be like to get up there, helpless in front of everyone.

"Yes, actually I do." Already her body hummed with anticipation. What better way to kick off the rest of her night than by putting herself out there in a new way?

"Come with me then and I'll get you set up."

She followed Gabe through the crowd as they headed for the cage in the middle of the room. The energy of it all vibrated through her core, turning her on. She'd certainly come a long way from the first night she'd stepped into the club. Gabe held his hand up and she allowed him to lead her onto the small stage.

Her stomach tightened, partly from nerves, but mostly excitement. She looked down at her outfit, grateful that she'd chosen to go bold and daring tonight. The miniscule leather skirt didn't quite cover her ass, and the fishnet halter-top allowed a peek at her nipples that were currently straining against the fabric.

"Raise your arms for me, Em." She did as he asked and he placed the manacles around her wrists, fastening her arms to the chains hanging from the top corner of the cage. Emerson spread her legs and allowed him to bind her ankles as well.

"You comfortable?"

She nodded.

Gabe stood back and appraised her appearance. "You picked the perfect outfit for tonight. If I didn't know better, I'd say you had something like this in mind to begin with." Heat flared in his eyes as he reached for the hem of her skirt. For a split second his fingers flirted with the seam of her ass before he rubbed his palms down the back of her thighs and up again, lifting her skirt to reveal her bare bottom and get the show started.

The crowd around her roared their approval as a shot of excitement rushed through her chest and straight to her core. Large, strong hands massaged her ass as her body writhed in tempo with his movements. God, she loved this. Her head buzzed with the rhythm of the music and the heady sensations of Gabe stroking her ass while everyone watched and chanted for more.

When Gabe pulled his hand away she didn't expect the loud smack across her skin that came next. The stinging pain caught her breath until his hand returned and smoothed the pain away.

"I'll bet your pussy's soaked right about now."

"Maybe." Hell yeah, she'd felt a liquid rush from the moment she'd stepped up to the platform.

"Ahh, darlin', your teasing days are over now, aren't they? If you stay for the private session, one of these Doms here tonight is going to show us all just how tasty you are."

Emerson's muscles jolted deep inside her. Gabe had no idea how much she longed to take her education and experience to the next level. As much as she wanted Rio to be the one to do it, she wasn't waiting for him anymore. It was now or never.

Another resounding smack on her opposite cheek brought her focus back to the here and now, and the crowd cheering in front of her. Automatically her hands fought at the bindings around her wrists, her mind shrieking for her to touch herself.

"Everyone in the VIP area is watching you right now. Speculating...planning. But don't worry. Dan came up with the perfect idea for your introduction tonight. Something more civilized than just fighting over you." Gabe's breath tickled the back of her neck every time he spoke, only increasing the madness building inside her—and he knew it.

"Who is watching me?" She couldn't see the area behind her and she didn't have the guts to ask him if Rio watched.

"Everyone." With a final smack to her ass, Gabe strode from the platform, leaving her body on fire and pulsating with the music. Just the way the patrons liked it.

Emerson bucked and swayed her hips to the beat of the music as the image of Rio standing behind her, staring at her, burned into her brain. This wouldn't be the first time he'd seen her naked butt in the club, but it was the first time she'd gone to the cage to be chained. From everything she'd heard, that's how he liked his submissives. Chained and helpless...

RIO WATCHED the mysterious Em's slender body sway with the music, her pale skin glowing in the ultraviolet lighting. His pulse pounded through his veins to the same tempo, and his dick pressed against his zipper so tight he thought he'd probably end up with a permanent imprint.

His fingers itched to trace the curved lines of her back, feel her sleek skin against his own. There were so many things he could do to her in that position, all designed to maximize her pleasure and feed on the energy of the crowd. If she were his, he would keep her like that as often as possible —on edge, ready.

For weeks he'd watched her grow downright daring, noting the clothes she wore to the play stations she visited, and how she finally allowed herself to be restrained in performance. Several times she'd caught him, and he could have sworn desire and something more had flared in her gaze—the same arousal he experienced every time he caught sight of her.

It was a shame he couldn't see her luminous eyes right now, although his imagination could envision them quite well. Slightly parted lips and flushed skin topped off with a look of longing not even he could deny. With each slow roll of her hips and tug on the cuffs at her wrists, his mouth watered and more blood rushed to his groin. She looked hot on display—every man in the place watched her with obvious lust in their eyes and thoughts in their heads of what they'd like to do to her.

Mine.

She threw her head back, arching her neck, and thrust her breasts toward the crowd. Fuck, the woman would have him crazed with longing before this little show was over. In that moment, he longed to stand behind her, feel between her legs, and see for himself just how wet she'd become. To whisper in her ear how he ached to fuck her. But he wouldn't do it, not before she begged.

What about her drew him so much? He'd heard through talk about her age, which made him uncomfortable and had been one of the main reasons he'd avoided talking to her. His needs ran dark, and from his past actions he'd learned the inexperienced weren't likely to fulfill them. Now, watching her stand there bound and open, he wondered if he'd been too hasty in his assessment.

From this view he could no longer see her hiding behind her mask. He ached to see more of her like this, free and naked, waiting for him.

Yeah, he had it bad when it came to Em, the secretive little minx who riled everyone up without even realizing it. Something tugged at the edge of his conscious as he surveyed the scene. Gabe stood not far from the stage, keeping vigil over her, probably dying to get a piece of her for himself.

So with all the interested players and her willingness to put herself out there, why the mask? What could she possibly be hiding that couldn't be revealed here? Purgatory was all about being yourself, free to be who you needed to be. Not to mention taking the opportunity to indulge in some fantasies, no matter how forbidden.

Time was ticking and his patience would only hold out so long. Soon he would have to find out.

CHAPTER 2

Twenty minutes later, Gabe returned and helped her down from the stage. Her legs and arms shook, and her pussy and nipples ached for attention. The fantasies she'd indulged in with the crowd watching left her ready to beg if she had to.

They crossed straight to the bar where Katie sat at one of the cocktail tables, waiting with a bottle of water.

"I've got her, Gabe, thanks."

"You sure? She's shaking pretty bad. She needs—"

"I've got her. Besides, you've got a club to close." Katie helped her to the chair and handed her the water. "Drink."

Em took the offered bottle and placed it to her lips, focusing on the cool water sliding down her throat and not the throbbing between her legs.

"You really get into that being on display thing, don't you?" Katie asked.

Emerson felt the heat creeping up her neck and onto her cheeks, but she wasn't really embarrassed. How could she be when her blood flamed with arousal and her head spun from the attention?

"Yeah, I guess so." She panted. "I didn't know—didn't know it would be that intense."

"You've had Rio on the brain all night and that little trip pushed you over the edge."

Katie kept talking, but Emerson zoned her out, only thinking about hot hands on her ass, which she could swear she still felt. The music had stopped for a few minutes while the announcement of the club closing was made, but now it had returned and while the volume was lower it still held a driving, rhythmic beat that pulsed to her clit.

What would Rio say if she bent over this table and begged him to fuck her right here, right now?

"Are you even listening to me, Em?" Katie's voice pierced her wildly running thoughts with her stern tone.

"I can't stop...the music...the atmosphere."

"It's called subspace, Em, and you've lost your own ability to control the moment."

"I need to—God, I don't know what the hell I need."

"Yes, you do. You need to fuck, to get off, and right now you don't even care with whom."

"Rio."

"Isn't here right now, and I'm not going to let you face him or the coming party like this."

Emerson laid her forehead down on the table and gulped for breath. The room needed to quit spinning.

"Em, do you trust me?"

"Of course I trust you."

"Enough to let me help you so you can recover?"

"Anything, please…" Soft fingers caressed her neck and massaged her shoulders. Katie was such a nice girl. Leo and Quinn better appreciate her.

She whimpered when Katie moved from behind her and took the seat next to her at the table.

"I'm going to touch you, Em, stay as calm as you can. Quiet, too, unless you want us both in trouble for sexual contact in a public area."

Em nodded. She'd do anything Katie wanted her to. Cool hands touched her inner thigh and the fingers traced a circle there, teasing her into relaxation.

"That feels good."

"I know it does, sweetie. Just trust me that I can help you and we'll have you back out there in time for the private festivities to begin."

Katie leaned into her until their bodies touched and Emerson relaxed into her soft, femininity. The scent of ripened raspberries hit her nose at the same time Katie's hand moved a few more inches up her thigh.

Awareness dawned and Emerson realized what would happen if she allowed Katie to keep going. Allowed, hell. Her body screamed to be touched, to find release any way it could get.

She raised her head to look at her friend and recognized arousal in her gaze as well as flushed cheeks and soft panting.

"Shhh. You don't have to say a word. In fact, I think the less that is said, the better."

Emerson nodded. She did trust Katie. She'd been kind and friendly to her since the first night, gently coaxing her to open up and relax. Showing her that at Purgatory all kinds were welcomed and accepted, no matter what.

She'd been envious of her at first, watching the way her two men doted on her even when they demanded her submission at times. The obvious love between them inspired her.

She wanted only one man, and no matter how she tried to purge him from her system, she couldn't. Tonight she would have him or not.

Emerson sucked in a deep breath when slender fingers grazed across her wet and swollen flesh, driving her closer to madness with each slow inch. Where she craved to be taken hot and hard, Katie moved at her own pace and took her time, drawing her into the action.

"Please Katie, more." Emerson buried her face into her friend's neck and inhaled deeply, loving the woman's clean and fruity scent.

"Don't worry, little one, we'll get there." Her voice took on a husky tone, giving away her own arousal. A fact she liked very much. She'd occasionally given thought to being with a woman, but had never been brave enough to explore it. Until now.

Emerson tilted her hips slightly, giving Katie better access to her sex, anxious for her soft touch to reach her clit.

"You are very impatient. I suspect that's going to get you into a little bit of trouble tonight. Patience is the toughest lesson to learn and always one of the first a Dom expects you to master."

She wanted to agree with Katie, but she really couldn't concentrate on the conversation with fingers moving between her pussy lips, increasing the tension already coiled tight within her.

Her breasts ached as well, and even the little strips of fishnet covering them was too much. She longed to be naked and splayed out, an offering to Katie's desires. What would Rio think if he saw her then? Would watching a woman get her off turn him on, or would he even notice?

God, she needed to get him out of her head. Why should everything she did be a reflection of Rio when he'd barely said two words to her here at the club, and little more than tease her when he saw her at home?

"Oh, hell." She moaned when Katie slipped her first finger inside her, pushing against the sensitive skin and nerve endings already hyper aware.

"Shhh, it won't do either of us any good to get kicked out of here tonight."

Emerson clamped her lips shut and gritted her teeth against the need to scream when Katie added a second finger and increased the tempo of her movements. When she curled them inside her and rubbed against her G-spot, she practically jumped from the chair.

Her body shook with the new onslaught of sensations, and her head spun further as a rush of pleasure pulsed through her.

"Em, I'm going to touch your clit and I want you to come for me without screaming or making a sound. Do you understand?" The whispered command alone nearly threw her over the edge as she shook her head furiously.

Katie's fingers rubbed across her sensitive spot three more times and Emerson's muscles clamped around them, holding off her release until Katie touched her clit.

Two fingers latched onto one of her tight nipples and pinched and tugged at the same time her thumb pressed against her pulsing clit, sending an overload of fierce sensations racking through her body. Her lips pressed tightly together, she buried her face tight against Katie's skin as the mind numbing orgasm ripped through her body.

Emerson rode the fingers fucking in and out of her as the pain at her breast expanded her pleasure. When the waves engulfing her finally subsided, the tension in her body slowly released and she melted against her friend.

The pain at her nipple disappeared and Katie's hand eased from her body. "You are a beautiful and responsive woman, Em, and if Rio doesn't recognize that tonight, I might have to kick his ass."

Em glanced across the club at Leo and Quinn packing their gear. "What about them?"

Katie laughed. "I'm sure they know exactly what I'm up to and if they don't then I shall have to tell them."

Just then Leo glanced up, his gaze settling on Katie. Em swore the heat between them could set the place on fire. "I think Leo knows."

"Yep, and I foresee a devil of a punishment later."

"Oh no. I didn't mean to get you intro trouble. Maybe if I talk to him."

Katie covered her hand. "Don't even go there. You're my friend and I'd do anything to help a friend. Even take a delicious, drawn out flogging followed by a hard fuck."

Emerson laughed and turned her head. "Thank you, Katie."

"It was my pleasure, sweetheart, but if you're feeling able we should probably go and get cleaned up before the auction begins."

Nerves jolted anew in her stomach. In a moment of desperation she'd agreed to a big unveiling and auction as her introduction to the private group. It sounded like such a good idea, but what if Rio didn't want to buy her for the night? Emerson shook the negative thoughts from her head. If Rio truly didn't want her even now, then tonight she would move on.

CHAPTER 3

Rio walked into the third floor ballroom to a flurry of action at the stage in the middle of the room. "What's going on here?"

Ben, his friend and know it all Dom, turned and smiled. "You haven't heard?"

"Obviously not."

"We're inducting a new submissive into the group tonight and she has agreed to be auctioned for public play."

"Who is it, and why am I hearing about this now?"

"Apparently it was decided at the last minute.

"And?" He wanted to know who.

"It's that hot little thing who always wears a mask. I think they said her name is Em."

His stomach tightened. "We don't allow masks on this floor."

"That's the beauty of the whole thing. She'll wear her mask for the auction and then the winner will reveal her identity."

Rio's cock perked up instantly at the remembered image of the masked Em in the cage tonight. Even in the smoky and darkened club he could make out her reddened cheeks from where Gabe had given her several good smacks on the ass as he'd worked her up for the crowd.

It wasn't the first time he noticed her, but her open and sensual response to the crowd tonight had really grabbed his attention. So far, she hadn't spent much time with any particular Doms at the club, but she had become braver each week with her clothing choices, and tonight she'd really opened up.

"What time is the auction?"

"Whenever the little honey gets that cute ass of hers up here." Ben moved in closer and lowered his voice. "I heard that her performance downstairs really got her off and she needed some help coming down."

"Some help?" He didn't like the sound of that.

"Yeah, Gabe offered his assistance but Katie pushed him away and took control of Em in the corner by the bar. I don't know what happened there, but boy, would I have enjoyed being a fly on the wall."

Rio nailed Ben with a hard glare. "You are such an ass sometimes."

"Yeah, and that's what the subbies love so much about me." He flashed a toothy grin. "Are you going to tell me that you aren't curious about what Katie did to bring Ms. Masked Hottie down from subspace?"

He was, but he wasn't about to share that with Ben or anyone else. When he didn't rise to the bait, Ben wandered closer to the auction floor as the crowd grew ever larger with anticipation. This was going to get interesting.

Gabe stepped up to the microphone and the noise in the room quieted down. "I know y'all have heard about the plan by now, so why don't we get our newest submissive in here and we can get this show on the road?"

Rio glanced at the door in the far corner and saw a small figure staring through a slight crack in the door. He'd bet the infamous woman of the hour was the one peeking in. He could imagine her standing there, biting her lip and tugging at the edges of her straight brown hair.

"The rules are pretty simple. We're doing this impromptu auction for the club's favorite charity and the beautiful Em has agreed to a public play scene within her club documented limits, of course."

A round of boos erupted from the crowd, followed by raucous laughter. Rio figured this little lady would fetch a pretty high price for the night.

"Oh, and don't forget at the close of the auction, the winning Dom will remove her mask right here on stage before any play begins in accordance with our club's policy."

Applause erupted, as did a few calls to get on with the show, and even Rio vibrated with an urgency he couldn't quite contain. He wanted to see who was behind that mask.

"You going to bid tonight, Rio?" Ben couldn't seem to let this situation go.

"Don't know yet. I think I'll wait and see what the rest of you pervs do."

"Takes one to know one, I reckon."

"I guess so." He liked that even though Ben came across goofy at times, he didn't get all puffed up and put out at the slightest perceived insult. He couldn't tolerate that kind of crap.

Gabe leaned into the microphone and turned his head to the door. "Katie, hon, go ahead and bring her in."

More applause sounded when the door swung open and Katie stepped through, leading Em by the elbow. Now those riggers were some damn lucky men when they'd latched onto Katie. She was the epitome of a Dom's wet dream with her tight corset that cinched her waist and lifted her ample breasts to almost spilling over the top. Even now with her flushed face and bright smile, she would be breaking hearts all over again.

But it was Em who continued to draw his eye, and had for sometime. He guessed she only stood five-two, which was a far cry from his six feet. Her slender body fit her height, but the first time she'd pulled her skirt up in the club for a flogging, she'd revealed a perfectly round ass that pinkened to a glowing red against her pale skin when spanked.

He'd yet to get close enough to see the color of her eyes, but the ruby red tint of her full lips mesmerized him, making him wonder what she tasted like.

Katie released her arm as Em took to the steps and made her way across the platform to stand next to Gabe.

"Hey, sweetheart, how are you doing?"

"Fine." She spoke quietly but the powerful microphone picked up her voice. Hesitant. Sweet. Familiar. A memory tugged at him that he couldn't quite reach. Where could he know this delicate morsel from, and how could he possible have forgotten her?

"All right, men, Em here is ready. So let's start the bidding at fifty dollars."

Right away a man up front raised his hand and the bidding rocketed from fifty to five hundred in under a minute. Apparently Em was a popular girl here at the club.

"Did you gentleman see our darling here in the cage tonight?" Gabe bent and trailed his fingers from her knee to the edge of her skimpy skirt and they all watched a shudder rack through her. "It's been a long time since I've seen such a natural in public. Someone here is going to be one lucky man tonight. In fact, I think I might be jealous."

Catcalls and lewd suggestions flew through the crowd as Gabe worked them up for more bidding. His gaze traveled back to Em and he found her staring at him, not moving or looking around. Rio's cock thickened at the intensity and the determination he saw there, a trait that called out to him in challenge. Her body language spoke of pride in who she was, and the slightly parted lips and tight nipples reminded him how much she liked the attention of a public setting.

"All right, settle down, or I'm just going to keep her for myself."

A slight smile formed at the edge of her lips but her gaze never wavered. Whatever happened from here on out, for whatever reason, she had set her sights on him. As the bidding raced toward one thousand dollars his dick continued to grow under her perusal and she didn't flinch or blink for a second from his.

"How about we sweeten the pot, fellas?" Gabe leaned into her and whispered something in her ear and she nodded, giving her consent to whatever it was he wanted to do.

He spun her around, forcing her to look away, and ordered her to bend over. Not only did that move reveal the globes of her ass, it also exposed a bare pussy when he nudged her legs farther apart. Someone in the crowd handed him a flogger, which he trailed lightly across each of her cheeks.

"For each bid you place, she will receive one stroke against her bare bottom." Quickly several men threw out bid numbers and she received several strikes one right after the other.

At fifteen hundred the bids once again slowed and Gabe stopped long enough for everyone to see the red streaks already forming and the moisture collecting along the swollen lips of her cunt.

Rio couldn't take it anymore. Everything in him wanted to be the one stroking the tender spots to soothe away her pain, to run his thick fingers through her slick folds until she begged him to end her torment.

"Two thousand dollars." His voice sounded broken but loud. Every head in the crowd turned to look at him. A few whispers broke out and Gabe stepped in front of the microphone asking for any more bids. Many of the men looked at each other and him, debating whether to bid against him. When no one stepped forward or spoke up, he declared Rio the winner of the night.

"Come and get your prize and let us all see what you have won."

Rio moved effortlessly through the parted crowd and hopped up onto the stage, moving to stand behind Em. As much as he couldn't wait to see her secret identity, he thought he'd play it up for the crowd. His fingers tugged at the secure tie holding her mask in place until it loosened. Her body stiffened and she held her breath.

"Don't worry, Em, this is what everyone has been waiting for." He pulled the mask away, letting it drop to the floor, and everyone in the room cheered.

"All right, everyone, the special auction is officially over. Let's play." Gabe strode from the stage and left him and Em standing together, waiting. Why all of a sudden had she frozen up, her back as stiff as a steel rod? She'd been playing to him as often as she could and tonight he'd finally bitten.

"Why are you so nervous?"

"I've been waiting for this for a very long time."

"The private party?"

"No." she hesitated and he waited. "You."

The newly formed pit in his stomach set off his instincts as alarms went off in his head. He was definitely missing something here. He jerked her shoulder and whipped her around, catching his first glimpse of her full face.

His heart stopped in his chest and blood pounded in his cock. His personal and very forbidden wet dream stood in front of him.

Emerson. Fuck.

CHAPTER 4

Emerson watched the rage build in Rio's eyes at her identity. She'd known this would not be easy but he looked like he might throttle her any second.

"What the fuck do you think you are doing, Emerson? Are you out of your mind?" he roughly whispered. Without giving her a chance to answer he grabbed her arm, his fingers digging into the flesh, and led her off the stage and into a small room off to the side.

She tried to jerk her arm out of his grasp, but he didn't let go. "What the hell does it look like I'm doing?"

"Playing games."

That stunned her. She hadn't thought he would be mean when he found out. Upset yes, mean no.

"I'm not playing any games, Rio. I'm an adult woman exploring her fantasies." She glared at him. "All of them."

His grip on her arm loosened and his thumb rubbed where he squeezed. The move seemed so automatic she wondered if he even realized he was doing it.

"You don't belong in a place like this."

"Why not? You're here."

"I'm not young and naïve, either." Oh, he went too far on that one. He needed to stop treating her like a kid.

"I may be younger than you, but I sure as hell am not naïve. Or innocent or pure or any other ridiculous label you want to put on me."

"Your brother will kill us both if he finds out we're here together. I can't do this." He pushed his hands roughly through his hair, frustration lines forming around his mouth.

"Give me a break. I'm not twelve years old anymore, so you can't just pat me on the head and send me away again. If you don't want to be my Dom tonight, if I repel you that much, I will find someone else."

In a flash his hands circled her waist and hauled her against him. Every last hard inch of his chest, torso, and pelvis pressed against her, including the hard cock in his pants. Her pussy creamed again, betraying her anger.

"You will not find someone else," he whispered darkly. His lips hovered near her mouth as she struggled for breath. He had the ability to twist her up and turn her around so that she couldn't remember who she was, let alone what she wanted to say.

"I'm not leaving." He'd better not force her hand on this, his influence in the club could very well get her expelled. He continued to glare at her as the warmth of his arousal spread across her bare stomach. She'd often wondered what it would be like to wrap her hands around his thickness, maybe even slide it into her mouth. He couldn't just walk away now, could he?

Suddenly his mouth covered hers, rough and demanding. His tongue pushed between her lips and swept through her mouth, throwing her further off balance.

The deeper they went, the more she felt every inch of his thick shaft pressing against her. Any more and she would melt into a puddle on the floor.

He tore his mouth from hers. "There is no one else here for you. I shouldn't even be touching you. But God help me I can't stop now."

She wet her lips, stroking the swollen flesh of her mouth. "Why do you have to stop?"

His tongue licked at her bottom lip and she opened on a sigh, drawing him into her mouth and sucking on his tongue lightly. Her arms lifted and wrapped around his neck, more of his heat searing into her skin. She had waited so long for this moment, and had been willing to do anything to be naked and underneath him.

"You're just a kid, Emmy." She cringed at the name he used for her when she was little. He was never going to get past the fact that he was older than her and best friends with her brother. It was a barrier he wouldn't cross no matter whether he wanted to or not. She fought against tears that burned behind her lids. She couldn't cry... wouldn't.

She curled her fingers around his shoulders and shoved him away. "If you don't want me then stop torturing me."

Heat flared in his eyes, shifting his demeanor a moment before he moved. "You think this is torture? You haven't seen anything yet, babe." He grabbed her hand and pulled her from the room right into the crowd of partygoers. They were met with cheers and comments that sent heat rushing to her cheeks. They were still looking to watch her play.

Fat chance of that at this point. She'd be lucky if he didn't grab her by the hair and throw her out of the club. Probably would call her brother, too.

"You're sure this is what you really want, Emerson?" He spoke close to her, his warm breath caressing the skin and tickling her ear. Her heart raced and her nipples poked at the abrasive fishnet fabric encasing them.

"I'm sure," she whispered. What did he have in mind, was he going to fuck her in front of everyone? Her stomach clenched. There was no one anywhere she trusted more than Rio, even if he hovered on the edge of a foul mood. He would never physically hurt her, although the odds of a broken heart on her part were pretty high.

He led her over to an open room in the corner, mumbling something about consequences she chose to ignore. There was a door that could be closed for privacy, but he left it open. The wall facing out to the ballroom would have been almost entirely a window had there been a window in it. Instead it was a big square hole where the crowd could gather and watch.

Inside, the room was painted midnight blue with soft lighting that gave visitors and players plenty of light to see without being harsh. Extraordinary black and white erotic photos hung strategically around the room and black cabinets sat in each corner, filled with any toy or implement one could think of.

In the center of the room stood a custom made, leather covered horse. A real showpiece bench made for many wicked delights, she imagined. Not to mention the pain that could be implemented if that was her desire. They headed in that direction and she pictured herself tied down on top of it with her naked ass facing the window.

Rio pulled her past it, though, and instead led her to the cross nailed to the wall that had a low bench in a wide V shape. "Are you familiar with one of these?" he asked her.

She shook her head as the picture formed. There were hooks at the ends of the cross and on the bottom of the ends of the narrow seat.

"It's called a St. George's chair, perfect for a wanton girl like yourself. Remove your clothing and have a seat."

She hesitated.

He leveled a serious look at her. "Emerson, are you going to be able to obey?"

She swallowed past the lump in her throat and settled her hands across her stomach to settle her nerves. "Yes, Sir." She untied her halter at her neck and back and let it fall to the ground at her feet. She then shimmied from her skirt and kicked it off her legs. Standing naked in front of him for the first time was both a thrill and nerve wracking. He paused a moment to look her up and down from head to toe, then headed over to the cabinet for supplies.

"Go ahead and sit."

Feeling slightly self-conscious, she did as told and turned and sat on the small seat with her back against the padded cross on the wall. When she looked up, she faced the open window and the huge crowd that had formed to watch. She'd heard their hushed whispers behind her back, but seeing them in front of her, not knowing how far Rio wanted to go, left her with a familiar nervousness tinged with excitement coursing through her veins.

He returned with several packages, which he placed on the table next to her. "Let me have your wrist." She held out her hand and watched him wrap her wrist with a black leather cuff lined with pink fur. He repeated binding her on the other side. Each cuff had a D-ring that attached to the fasteners at the far end of each side of the cross, so that her arms were straight out and basically attached to the wall.

"Ankles, now." He stood in front of her, temporarily shielding her from the crowd. His big hands caressed her knees while his mouth took her in a slow, drugging kiss. Em opened to him, hungry for what he gave. What surprised her was the obvious show of need from him with each thrust of his tongue. His passion took her breath away. She could get lost in attention like this. With her focus solely on his possession of her mouth, she barely noticed that his hands slid between her thighs and pushed her legs open until the cool air rushed across her now exposed labia. She moaned into his mouth, and he swallowed the needy sound.

He broke the kiss and went to work attaching her legs to the bottom of the chair. When he finished, he stood and walked to the table at her side. She now sat fastened down with her arms and legs spread open, her pussy on complete display to all who watched. There were many smiles and appreciative gestures in her direction and, despite her love for attention, her body heated.

"Emerson, look at me." She turned and met his gaze. "Are you frightened?"

Was she? She was certainly nervous but no, not scared.

"No."

Rio smiled that wicked grin, the one that said, I am going to devour you. "How did I know you were going to enjoy this?" He picked up a black cloth from the table and draped it across his hands. "You've been hiding from all of us for months, I think it's only fair that we hide from you this time." He wrapped the blindfold around her eyes, tying it in the back. Her hands strained against her restraints in automatic response to wanting to remove the blindfold.

"Are you sure you trust me, sweetheart?" The deep cadence of his voice relaxed her struggling. Of course she trusted him. She'd known him since she was a pre-teen with a silly crush.

"Yes, of course."

"You are a very brave girl." Without seeing his face she couldn't tell whether he was being sarcastic or not. She suspected he was.

With her vision removed, her other senses began to take up the slack. The voices at the window seemed to grow louder and she even heard Rio's deep but quickened breathing. She'd bet he was as excited by this event as she was. She longed to see his reactions, to touch his body, to know what he was thinking.

"Loss of control is hard for a first timer in a situation like this, so my job is to break through the barriers you are building and give you what you need. Like these breasts...so petite and succulent...and in great need of attention."

His hands massaged and stroked her small globes. When his fingers grazed her nipples she arched her back into his hands with a hiss of pleasure. With forefinger and thumb he pinched her tips until she sucked in a hard breath. Pain built alongside the pleasure.

"Try to be still for me, Emerson. This is all about control for both of us. You still have a lot to learn."

How could she be still when every touch and taste was designed to drive her crazy? She whimpered when his hands left her body and he moved away. The whispers of the crowd returned without him there to distract her. She made out the words tits and cunt several times. Liquid heat rushed to the folds of her pussy. God, even if she wanted to deny how much this turned her on, the evidence gave her away.

A new sound came from the direction of the little table and she realized that Rio had moved the stool she'd seen along the wall. Was he sitting on it? Would he be touching her again?

"Everyone loves your body, sweetheart. They want more...they want to see you come." Her head jerked at the close contact of his voice in her ear. She hadn't even heard him approach. "Do you want more? Or should I stop now and let you go?"

"No, don't stop." Her voice came out hoarse and louder than she'd expected, and a murmured appreciation came from the end of the room. A light stroke of her flat belly sent new shivers racing to her core.

"Relax, Emerson. You're supposed to enjoy yourself." She loved the dark timbre of his voice, it soothed her and allowed her to slowly release the tension in her shoulders and torso. When his fingers trailed through the wet slit of her sex, she tried to tilt her hips to encourage him and received a sharp slap to her inner thigh.

"You're not being still like I asked. Patience is what you need."

"Can't help it, need so much." She breathed heavily.

"I know, and you need to trust me that I understand these things. Trust me, Emerson. In fact, I am revoking your permission to speak. You will also have to remain quiet. Do you understand?"

She nodded. "Good girl. Now let me give everyone a good view of this pretty pink pussy of yours."

His fingers moved quickly, spreading her lips wide open. Besides the few whispers she heard, she also caught a few moans, both feminine and masculine.

"It's very lickable, wouldn't you say?" Her muscles clenched tight and her juices flowed at his words. She had longed to know what it would feel like to have Rio's mouth there, teasing her clit...tasting her.

The stool moved rapidly like it had been kicked out of the way, but she had no idea what he was doing. Footsteps...she heard several. Only Rio's, or were there others as well? His hands dropped away and she heard a package being opened on the table. Every muscle in her body had gone taut, unable to relax as she tried to anticipate his next move and the next touch to her body.

"I think this toy will be a good way to really get this part started." A buzzing noise started up and she knew he held a vibrator of some sort.

"Hold this for me, will you? And feel free to give it a little test run on her if you like while I get the next implement ready."

Who the hell was he talking to? He wanted someone else to play with her as well? She didn't get much chance to think about it when the cool, vibrating toy was pushed against her nipple. The low buzz sparked a reaction deep in her body and the whimpers she'd managed to hold back came tumbling out.

"Very nice. I think she likes that." Another package opened as the vibrations went from one nipple to the other until the peaks tightened almost painfully. She heard a vague squirting noise in the distance and then a finger was touching her ass, poking at the small hole. She hadn't even realized the chair had left that part of her anatomy accessible.

"I'll bet you've never been taken there, have you?" Oh, God—the slick finger breached her hole and pushed against untouched nerve endings. "That's okay. I have just the thing to help that virgin ass." His finger pushed in a little farther and then withdrew. A gasp tore from her mouth at the change in sensation. Holy hell.

"Now, do your best to relax and push against the plug if you can. It will make getting it in all the easier." A cool, rigid shape pushed against the puckered hole Rio had lubricated in preparation. She sucked in a breath and relaxed on the exhale. She could do this.

Suddenly the vibrator was removed from her breasts and placed lightly across her clit, sending shards of pleasure streaking through her body as the plug slid into place in her ass, stretching and filling her.

"Oh, such a good girl you are. I think you deserve a reward." He snapped his finger and moments later a mouth latched onto each one of her breasts. She was quickly losing count as to how many people touched her. Now, teeth bit at her nipples just enough to give her that edge of pain that heightened the feel of the vibrator at her clit and the plug seated in her ass.

"You've become quite the star tonight, Emerson." She couldn't focus on his words. Sensations and pressure built inside her to the point she couldn't stop it. Her legs and arms shook with the need to come. Knowing that everyone in the room and at the window would watch only heightened her pleasure. With anyone else she might have backed out, but Rio would take care of her, she knew.

"Make me come, Rio. Please, I need you, please." She pleaded with him, wanting him to be the one to tip her over the edge. Her heart raced in the silence of the room as she struggled to wait for him. "Please," she whimpered.

When she'd about given up the fight, fingers plunged into her slick vagina. She thought she'd heard Rio swear but she couldn't be sure as the shocking arousal ratcheted higher than anything she'd ever experienced. In and out those fingers moved, spearing her, rubbing tissues already aroused until the combination of it all exploded in her body.

Muscles spasmed uncontrollably as her body jerked in response. Screams ripped from her throat and bounced around the room as the darkness enveloped her, leaving her shocked and shaken at the force of her release.

Cheers and applause erupted around her and Rio hastily removed her blindfold.

"Are you okay, Em?"

She blinked against the lights and focused in on his face in front of her. Unable to speak, she only nodded. Her head slumped forward and Rio caught her with his hands.

"It's okay, sweetheart, I've got you." Fingers pawed at the cuffs of her wrists and ankles and she opened her eyes again to see Gabe and Katie setting her free. When her body was loose, Rio scooped her into his arms and held her tight against his chest. His lips pressed against her forehead in a gentle caress.

"Show's over, folks. We need our privacy." With that he carried her through the archway that led to a private bedroom with no windows and closed the door behind him.

Her mind reeled from the emotions coursing through her as Rio laid her out on the bed. She'd been surprised to see Gabe and Katie sharing the scene with her, but grateful for it. Much better than with strangers.

He rubbed at all the sore spots from their session. First, his thumbs caressed the skin around her wrists in a light circular motion while the smooth slide of his tongue tormented the soft skin of a breast.

Through hooded eyes Em watched Rio trail his fingers along her sides to the tight muscles of her thighs. His head lowered to nibble his way from her breast to her belly button where he dipped his hot tongue and swirled through the indention. All the while he worked magic with his hands, massaging her muscles until she practically melted into the bed.

"Do you know how wonderful you are? Precious even?" Rio couldn't stop touching her despite his best intentions. The shock at seeing her in Purgatory still took him by surprise, even more so after the scene they'd just done. She'd taken to it like a fish to water, which wouldn't have surprised him if it wasn't his Emerson.

His Emerson. Like it or not that's how he'd thought of her for a long time now. Sure, she'd had an obvious crush on him as a teenager, and he'd grown protective over her because of it. But ever since she'd returned from college, it had been his turn to lust after her, and he'd felt guilty about it.

Not only was there a pretty big age gap between them, there was the fact that as his best friend's sister that put her clearly in the do not touch *ever* category.

So much for that plan.

Lying next to her now, soothing her back to reality, his erection throbbed to be inside her. Something that wasn't about to go away.

"How are you now, Em, feeling better?"

"I felt fine before, I just needed some privacy to relax, but now I need—" She hesitated.

"You need what?" She didn't have to speak the words for him to know but he really wanted to hear her say it.

"I need you, Rio. I need you inside me. I need to know this is real."

"Oh, it's real all right." His fingers slid between her legs into her slick heat to find her hot and ready. She had no idea how bad his belly trembled with the desire to be buried inside her. To have her legs wrapped around him as she screamed in ecstasy when he made her come. His hand stilled. "If you don't want to go through with this, you need to tell me now. This changes everything and if we go any further, I don't think I could stop."

She tilted her hips in his hand so he cupped her sex. "I don't want you to stop." She stared back at him with determination and desire in her eyes. "I want you to take me."

Her words ignited the fuse that exploded his control. He grabbed her wrists and shoved them above her head, holding her there with one hand while his fingers rubbed at her clit until she whimpered next to him. He couldn't play anymore, couldn't wait another second to have her wet tightness sucking him inside.

He moved over her and gripped her wrists tighter, locking her into place, and crushed his mouth to hers. Her taste, smooth like a fine wine, drove him over the edge until his knee nudged her legs farther apart and his swollen tip hovered at her entrance.

Ripping his mouth from hers, he gazed down at her flushed face. Those swollen ruby lips still beckoned, but he had to hear her say it one more time. "Tell me, Em, tell me again."

With no hesitation she looked at him and spoke. "Take me, please," she moaned.

The smooth, wet skin of her pussy teased him as he parted her folds with his shaft. Agony swept through him as he tried to go slow and not hurt her. She was a tiny thing.

"Hurry, Rio, I need more." Her pleading words did him in as he unleashed the force of his need and drove to his balls in one smooth thrust.

Rio drew back, leaving just the tip at her entrance before once again plunging deep. Emerson's legs squeezed his sides when her hips bucked upward. In and out he repeated, her nails digging into his arms and back on each thrust.

Harsh breathing blending with moans and grunts drove his passion and need to a frenzy.

Take me. Take me. He heard her command in his head over and over as her muscles tightened and his balls drew tight against his skin, tingling with the beginning of his release. She was forbidden and he'd taken her anyways, and now he needed more. Needed it all.

Her sex spasmed around him with her orgasm as she let loose a scream that filled the room, and likely the club. He withdrew once more as the powerful wave of lust and satisfaction surged over him and into her. Muscles rippled and shuddered as he continued to pump into her until replete, then he collapsed over her.

Their hearts beat together in a race to catch their breath as the implications of what they'd done crashed into him. He would definitely have some explaining to do. He didn't want to lose his best friend, but Em was important to him. He wanted her as his girlfriend, his submissive. Hell, probably more.

Realizing he was crushing her petite frame, he slipped from her body and rolled from the bed. Stepping into the nearby bathroom, he grabbed a soft cloth and soaked it in hot water, and returned to her.

Her gaze tracked him, careful and cautious. She looked nervous.

"Please don't tell me that you regret what happened." Her voice came out soft and anxious, maybe afraid.

He blew out a harsh breath and a hard sigh. "No, Em, not regret."

She sat up quickly and moved to the other side of the bed, dragging the sheet around her body since she had no clothes in the room.

"Where are you going?"

"I'm leaving before you break my heart." She stumbled in the bedding and he rushed the corner of the bed, blocking her exit.

"You're not leaving."

"Yes. I am. I saw your face, heard the resignation in the sigh. I know what comes next and I'd rather not hear it."

Tears leaked from her eyes and tore at his heart. She'd misunderstood. "Not only are you not leaving tonight, if I have anything to say about it, you may never leave."

She stopped dead in her tracks, her head bowed to the floor. Seconds ticked by and she didn't move, only the sound of her breathing filled the room.

"Em, look at me." His fingers reached for her chin and tipped her head back so that her moist eyes were again visible to him. She really did look different without the mass of curls surrounding her face. She'd become quite the chameleon.

"Your brother may hurt me for this, but I'm not letting you go. That's if you'll still have me."

She hesitated for several minutes before a sly grin worked its way across her face. The sheet dropped and she jumped into his arms laughing and kissing at his neck and shoulders until they tumbled together on the bed.

"I'll take that as a yes."

"Are you crazy? Do you know how long I have waited for this day? Of course it's a yes."

Her nipples pressed against his chest and he couldn't resist reaching between them to tweak one of them. He wanted them in his mouth again, the tender tips between his teeth until she shrieked for him to stop. He was so going to enjoy testing her limits.

"You do realize this changes everything between us? I'm hard enough to live with as a friend, but as a Dom..."

"I've heard the stories." She pushed her fingers through his hair. Fresh lust kicked him in the gut. The look on her face...

"Well, take what you've heard and multiply it by ten and maybe you'll hit the extent of what I have planned for you."

"Whatever you want, Rio," she whispered.

"Don't go making promises your butt can't cash sweetheart."

Rio locked his arms around her and flipped her over until she lay underneath him, belly down.

"But I'll take it as a start." Despite the amazing orgasm he'd just had, his cock began to stir. If he had his way, and he would, there would be many more even bigger orgasms through the rest of this night. Standing up, he rubbed the pearly cheeks of her ass before letting one of his hands fall with a good hard smack.

She gasped and swiveled her head. "What was that for?"

A wicked grin spread across his face. "I think it's time for your next lesson."

Thank you so much for reading!

Want to learn about Cass and Walker in TEASED, next in the Purgatory Club series?

Continue reading for the full first chapter of TEASED, which is available now.

If you haven't read all of the books in my Purgatory Club series or the Purgatory Masters, you can find the full reading order and links at EMGAYLE.com

Join Eliza's VIP newsletter at emgayle.com/news and be the first to be notified of new releases, sales and contests.

If you're on <u>Facebook</u> or <u>Twitter</u>, come by and say hello! I'd love to hear from you.

If you enjoyed reading this story, please consider leaving a review on your favorite retailer?

Just a few words and some stars really does help!

Continue reading for a full booklist and the complete Chapter One of TEASED, the next book in the Purgatory Club series.

COMPLETE CHAPTER 1

The slap of leather against naked flesh echoed in Walker's brain, tormenting his need, which was already at a feverish level. He stepped, mindless, from the club into the harsh, biting wind. A few die-hard smokers huddled close to the wall, the glowing embers of their addiction lighting the darkened patio. He wasn't a smoker, but it was the only place outside to catch his breath and maybe relocate the section of his brain where his control was stored.

He'd spent the last hour at the flogging station with Dex, watching and waiting—for what, he wasn't sure. There had been a steady stream of beautiful women in line waiting to get flogged by the most popular Dom in the club, but when the cadence of blows began to beat in rhythm with the pulse in his stiff dick he decided it was time to get some fresh air.

"Hey man, you gotta light?" One of the half naked, leather and black nail polish goth guys ambled over to him.

"No, don't smoke." And he wanted to be left alone.

Goth Boy gave him a confused look before he turned and wandered back to his group.

What am I doing here?

He'd moved to town six months ago after a long and difficult break up. By chance he'd overhead some clients talking about Purgatory and, his curiosity piqued, he'd come to check it out. It had been everything he'd expected, plus so much more. The club seemed to cater to a variety of clientele from the straight goth crowd to the extreme fetishists, and the place was definitely a playground for the voyeur. Drawn to the upstairs VIP area and its many play stations, he came here as often as he could get away.

Lately, though, simply observing wasn't enough, and the few times Dex had handed him the flogger to take over when he needed a break had been very nice. What he craved, although, ran much deeper than flogging a stranger. There were willing and available submissives in the club he could play with, but he yearned for a connection and a level of submission he doubted most women here would understand. Besides, he hated the word play, and the first time it came out of a sub's mouth he was usually gone.

Walker pulled his collar around his neck and shivered in the cold. He couldn't stay out here much longer, so it was either go back inside or head on home. At least now his body was under a semblance of control. A glance at his watch showed ten-thirty, still early for a Saturday night.

Fine. He'd go in and watch a few of the stations, chat with Dex, then head on home.

Alone. Again.

Walker pulled the heavy door open and hustled inside, seeking the awaiting heat and excitement. Bonnie, the door supervisor, smiled at him, and he returned a warm greeting.

"Walker, Sir, I can't believe you're out there without a jacket."

He'd chatted with her many times and found her as genuine as they came.

"I'd tell you again to just call me Walker, but you aren't ever going to do it are you?" She'd lost her Dom last year to cancer, and while she seemed to be embracing life once again she'd firmly stood against finding another man.

She blushed and lowered her gaze. "No, Sir."

He understood her grief and knew that one day someone worthy would come along and get her back on her knees where she so loved to be.

"No worries, Bonnie, I can see what a good girl you are and would certainly never hold that against you. No one should." He touched her chin and tilted her head until their gazes met. "It is chilly outside, so be sure to bundle up before you go home tonight." He liked the fact that he was getting to know everyone here and making friends. It never hurt to be around like-minded people who accepted him as is with no judgment.

A slow smile spread across her face and she nodded before turning her attention to the customer who'd come through the door behind him.

Glancing down on the main floor, he saw the rope swing in motion with Leo astride his latest victim as they swung from one end of the room to the other. The crowd went wild as the pretty blonde's face bloomed in ecstasy at the attention.

The club was in full Saturday night swing as he moved slowly through the crowds around each play station. He couldn't even get close enough to the extreme booth to see what they were currently offering up, so he turned and set off in the direction of the flogging stations.

By now his friend would be looking to take a break, but Walker wasn't sure he was up to wielding anymore tonight. Already his groin ached enough to give him second thoughts to any offers he might receive. He could use a good dick sucking right about now.

Kat and Cindi were busy marking the hell out of a couple of subbie boys when he walked up. Their arms arched back and sprang forward with as much force as they could find. The whoosh of the air splitting for the dozens of knotted tails caught and held his attention as they connected with bare, red streaked skin.

Dex stood next to him, watching and enjoying the show those ladies loved to put on. Every male subbie in the room ate it up and no doubt wished it was them like it was nobody's business.

"They've got some real pain sluts in the booth tonight," Dex mumbled.

"That's for sure. A little different from what you've got going on, huh?"

"Wait until you meet my next appointment, Cass. She's—"

"She's what?" A sultry sexy voice sounded behind them and both men jerked around to see.

"Why, she's the most beautiful woman in the room, that's what."

"Nice save, Dex," she murmured.

Walker stood speechless at the sight before him. Long, raven dark hair framed a narrow face, and dark eyes surrounded by thick inky lashes that watched him curiously. Her nose was ordinary but the red lips underneath drew him like a moth to flame. He lingered there watching them part slightly while her tongue darted to the edge. He felt his cock stir in his pants as his own curiosity piqued.

"Cass, here for another session, I see? Do you need to feel my flogger on your skin?" Dex teased her until she broke the look between them to turn to his friend.

"Need is overrated these days, Dex, you know that. But I can't deny I do enjoy coming to see you on occasion. Even a girl like me enjoys a little fun now and then."

Dex snorted and shook his head.

Walker closed his eyes and let her smoky voice float over him. There was more to what she said, he could sense it. The slight hitch in between sentences, the nervous way she moved her hands, all combined to make him curious to know who this Cass was and the story behind her.

"Well come on, sugar, you're in luck. You're next on my list." He led her to his station and waited for her to get in place.

A sexy ass swayed in a tight, low-slung denim skirt when she moved. Her outfit was a far cry from the leather and PVC wear of many in the crowd, but somehow the simplicity of denim riding low on her hips and a crisp, white cotton half-shirt leaving her midriff bare did more for him than all the big tits with their nipples covered by tiny strips of electrical tape. No, he was an ass man through and through, and the more she twitched it the more he thought about fucking it.

She had the art of teasing down to a fine science, and obviously she and Dex played this game regularly. He, however, was not a man to toy with unless you were fully prepared to follow through. He was more worked up than he had a right to be, but that didn't change the fact his body had come to life the moment he'd heard her voice.

Walker watched her. Slender fingers lifted to the buttons of her blouse and made quick time easing them each free. His heart raced with no other explanation than excitement at something or someone new. With her hands gripping the edges of the shirt, her head tilted up and her gaze connected with his.

He easily recognized the uncertainty in her eyes as well as the caution she directed at him, but underneath those surface reactions he saw the hunger. Gut deep, aching need crying out for relief. That very look would be what he thought of later tonight when he was jacking off again.

"Did you all of a sudden develop a case of shyness, Cass?" Dex winked at her and smiled.

"Don't be silly, I'm just enjoying the moment." Her eyes cleared in a split second.

"Uh huh."

She turned and faced the large St. Andrew's Cross filling Dex's space and jerked her shirt from her shoulders. More creamy skin and a flash of a white lace bra cupping high breasts filled his view for a few seconds before she settled her front against the smooth wood of the cross.

Besides the slim straps of her bra and the small skirt, Cass stood naked with her arms stretched above her along the lines of the wood. Walker stared, mesmerized by the expanse of tanned skin peeking from underneath the long fall of hair that touched the tip of a tribal tattoo on her lower back. Someone else might look at her mark and refer to it as her tramp stamp, but to him it seemed sexy, even sensual.

Dex whispered at her ear, low enough so only she heard as his hands deftly buckled her wrist into the leather cuff at the top. A moan sounded from her at whatever he said and her hips wiggled against the wood. This was going to be very interesting.

Dex glanced at him as he walked to her other side, revealing a heat that surprised him. Of all the floggers in the club he always remained cool and detached. Until now.

Dex stepped close, closer than necessary to get to her other hand and Walker couldn't miss the bulge in his pants as he did. A swift desire to pull him away from her and take over welled deep in his gut. Why he suddenly wanted to protect her made no sense. Dex was the best in the club and would care for her better than any Dom he'd ever seen. Still, his fists clenched tight at his side to keep from grabbing him and hauling him away.

"Walker, you okay?"

"Yeah." Except for the desire to wipe the knowing grin from his friend's face.

"I've never seen Cass react like that before I've even started. She holds onto that control of hers with an iron fist."

"Why is that?"

"There's a history there she doesn't want anyone to know. About six months ago she started coming in twice a month like clockwork. She's always friendly and eager, but it's not hard to see that she holds back."

"Interesting."

"It is, isn't it?" Dex had turned back to Cass as his question faded into their surroundings.

While he went to pick the right flogger, Walker moved to the side of the booth so if Cass turned her head he would see her face. He wanted to watch her reactions. Already her breathing appeared slightly labored as she anticipated the session. Every few breaths she took her body trembled, causing his to tighten further until he was as strung out as she.

He wanted her and, unless he missed his guess, which he rarely did when it came to reading people, so did Dex.

The session began with a simple suede flogger consisting of a multitude of long tails and various knots that Dex used to trail across her arms and back until a soft "please" fell from her lips. A sign the little sub was getting desperate for more.

He wanted to be the one coaxing the pleasure from Cass, but it would be awkward, to say the least, to ask for permission to do so. So instead he remained on the sidelines, rigid with need and longing for a woman who wouldn't even be described as pretty by others, but to him had become the most sensual creature he'd seen in a very long time.

"I know, baby. It's coming."

Dex talked to her in hushed tones that no one besides the three of them could have heard. As he raised his arm and delivered the tails across her back in a sharp blow, the sounds and people around them faded away. All of the focus was on Cass and her pleasure, fulfilling the need she'd come to Purgatory for.

Wrists twisted and turned so the tails moved in a sideways figure eight, and light pink marks began to appear across the skin of her back. Even while watching the flogging from the corner of his eyes Walker didn't take his gaze from the profile of her face. He willed her to turn and look at him, desperate to see her every reaction to his friend's superior skills.

As the falls to her backside increased, her hands clenched and unclenched into tights fists as she automatically pulled against her bindings. She'd been given a safe word to use if at any time the flogging became too much for her, but based on her body language she wouldn't be using it anytime soon.

Walker glanced at Dex to see his friend lost in concentration, his hand flipping the flogger both expertly and automatically as he watched for any sign of distress or pleasure on her part. On a loud moan from Cass, Dex looked over with a shit-eating grin stamped on his face. The man took pride in his ability to mold every submissive in his care to the perfect writhing ball of pleasure.

When Walker turned back to Cass, he caught her staring at him. Their gazes met and held and her lips parted, a moan rolling out and over him. His stomach seized as the need emanating from her melded with his, driving them both to the precipice of no return. With little thought to their surroundings his palm rubbed over his dick, pushing the seam of his pants into the sensitive skin. If she kept looking at him like that he was going to come in his fucking pants like a horny teenager.

Energy buzzed through his veins, as his innate need to be in control fought for dominance over the situation. He had to fight the urge to snatch the flogger from Dex and whip her until she begged to come for him.

Dex halted his movements and moved to the wall obviously looking to make a switch. Her pleas to not stop tore at his resistance as he took another step toward the platform. Dex chuckled from the other side, probably amused by his behavior but Walker was far beyond caring what anyone though of him at the moment.

This woman had managed to drag him in and pull him out of the shell he'd been waiting in. He'd decided actively looking was a waste of his time and other than his minor activities here at the club he'd buried his need for more.

Until tonight, when he'd seen her.

Tears rolled down her cheek as she watched him, her hips pressing into the cross. She was so close to her orgasm she'd resorted to rubbing that clit of hers against the edge of the wood in a desperate attempt to finish what Dex had started.

"If you come before he's finished, I'll make sure you're punished." The harsh command tumbled from Walker's mouth before his brain even considered them. He had no rights here, yet he couldn't help himself, he had to take charge.

Her sobs halted and her eyes widened in surprise. Seconds stretched out as she stared at him and he waited for the sassy retort he knew lingered on her tongue. Dex had returned to his place behind her and waited as well. He'd obviously overhead his statement and hesitated giving her a chance to respond.

On a long exhale she finally spoke. "Yes, Sir."

The tightness in his chest released, as did the breath he hadn't realized he'd been holding. He nodded to Dex, who stepped closer this time with two new floggers. With the flick of both wrists the leather tails wrapped around her thighs, under her skirt and perilously close to her cunt. He'd not struck hard but it'd been unexpected, and the wild look in her eyes pleased him.

"Tell him," Walker ordered. This time she didn't hesitate.

"More please, Dex. I need more." Her whispered voice hitched when she spoke.

He didn't take his eyes off of her as Dex increased the tempo of leather slapping against flesh and denim as he covered every inch, from her calves to the bare shoulders he itched to soothe.

Dex got back into the zone and Cass trembled and moaned with every touch. The sound of her arousal neared peak as her hips jerked forward, looking for anything to rub in her desperate attempt to increase the friction against her clit.

Walker not only wanted to bring her to the edge himself, he wanted to hold her there a little longer. With her chained to his wall without clothes, he could test and tease her until she exploded from overload. Everything inside told him she would respond to his brand of control, even thrive under it.

"Walker." Dex's voice broke into his thoughts, forcing his focus on this scene not the future. The subtle nod from his friend was all the encouragement he needed.

Walker moved, eating up the little distance left between Cass and himself. With his head bent and his lips close to her ear, heat rose from her skin, drawing him in.

"Cass, I know what you need. You want someone to direct, to give their permission, to allow you to come. But I'm not inclined to give it unless you ask for it." In reality he didn't care if she begged this time. He wanted to watch her come from the flogging, with little else for stimulation.

"Please." The words trembled from her mouth. "I have to come."

He begged to differ, but she obviously had a plan and they didn't know each other at all—except in the way that like always knows like, and this little sub had a deep dark need she was afraid of. The least he could do was not get in her way of satisfaction. Which, of course, had nothing to do with him wanting to see her writhing in ecstasy in front of the crowd.

He glanced at Dex, who delivered the final strike to her sides, the long leather tails wrapping around her inner thighs and delivering a swift pop against her clit. The nub he now imagined swollen and hard, waiting for the attention it deserved.

A long scream, drowned out by the throbbing industrial music, tore from her mouth. Her head fell back, her hair shaking loose and her hands yanking frantically on the bonds that held her in place.

Walker couldn't keep his hands off of her. His fingers settled on her waist, her muscles clenching underneath as she rode the wave of pleasure Dex —and maybe he in some small part—had created for her. Silky strands of hair brushed against his burning skin like a gentle wave of water on a hot day.

God, he wanted to tear off her panties, bury his head between her legs, and lap up every bit of cream she spilled. She'd be so fucking wet and hot, his dick jerked with the thought of it. If she thought this climax was good, he'd show her much better with his tongue.

As she came back down, he listened to the harsh breaths in and out of her lungs. Little aftershocks rippled across her body while Dex unfastened one arm and then reached for the other. With her wrists loose, she began to slump, and Walker scooped her into his arms and carried her to the sofa in the corner.

He cradled her to his chest, allowing her the time she needed to recover as well the time he needed to get his body and mind back under control. She was not his. Hell, he didn't even know her. Yet the intoxicating scent of vanilla mixed with her sexual musk seared into his brain, never to be forgotten.

She stirred in his lap, her eyes fluttering but not opening. Her skin glistened with a gentle pink flush, lips slightly parted as her breathing slowed to normal.

"Stop staring at me, you're making me uncomfortable," she whispered.

"I can't help it. I'm not sure I've ever seen anything so delectable."

Her eyes popped open—pools of ocean blue stared up at him, a look so intense yet laced with sorrow. She twisted away from his chest, her feet moving to the floor.

"You don't have to lie to me, it's unnecessary. I'm not a fool, you know." She rushed to her things and redressed quickly.

Anger radiated from her as the soft submissive look disappeared, the mask of a woman unaffected replacing it. Taken aback by her outburst, he said nothing, unsure what had happened.

Staring daggers at him, she spoke to Dex. "As always, Dex, you are the master of Purgatory. Thank you."

The last two words were spoken softly and without sarcasm before she turned on her heels and rushed into the crowd of the club. Walker warred with himself on whether to go after her or not. Everything about her screamed his, even the temper. Yet, right now she needed space. Time to recover. He'd have preferred in his arms, but there would be a next time he was certain.

"What the hell was that all about?" Walker turned to face his friend in time to see the mocking smile plastered across his features.

"The funniest thing I've seen in a long time, I'd say." Dex shook his head and picked up his cleaning spray and towel and proceeded to begin the wipe down of the cross before the next in line came for their turn.

"This is not funny, Dex. That woman is amazing, but she's in no condition to be wandering around by herself." He tried to catch a glimpse of her through the people crowded together but she'd disappeared from sight.

Dex turned back, his eyes narrowed. "Cass is a complicated woman, Walker. As a submissive she's had her heart torn out."

"What happened?" He'd better hear the story sooner rather than later so he knew what he was dealing with.

Dex's shoulders sagged as he finished cleaning up and hung the floggers on their hooks. His reluctance to continue did little to dissuade him as he waited for an answer. Time passed and Cass got farther away, possibly even gone for the night. He would have to rely on Dex to fill him in.

"There's something about her, Dex. Something that reached out to me like nothing has in a really long time." He was taking a chance on revealing his own secrets to his friend, but if he wanted information then he'd do what he had to in order for him to understand.

"I'm not blind, I saw how you reacted to her and how she reacted to you as well. I've been doing this a damn long time and thousands of submissives have passed through here with every story you could think of and then some." He picked up the clipboard and consulted the sign ups before he dropped it back on the small table. "Cass has been coming in for months and it's taken a while to get even half her story, and most of that from rumors around the club not from the woman herself."

Walker nodded. He liked that Cass had not been an easy read or willing to open up to any Dom who would listen. He had so many questions for Dex, but he knew him well enough to know that he needed to be patient. He would reveal what he wanted to when he was good and ready.

"From what I understand, she lived as a twenty-four-seven slave for some time until about a year ago when her Dom up and disappeared. As in packed up and left town without a word, leaving her to find out when she returned to an empty house one day after work."

Walker rubbed at his chest, annoyance already pressing down on him.

"Why?"

"No idea. For that answer you'd have to ask the lady herself, and so far I haven't been given an opening into her life for even the first personal question." Dex's fingers absently stroked the tails of his favored suede flogger as he spoke. "I think she's been trying to withdraw from the lifestyle for a while now, but every few weeks she shows up for a flogging, desperation written all over her face despite that pretty smile she fools everyone with."

Walker nodded in understanding. He and Dex were more alike than he'd thought. They'd both seen through the wall she'd built up to protect herself.

"A fucking shame if you ask me. Her need is palpable when she walks into the room. She's afraid to even try to open up to anyone, but that fear will never erase what her soul clamors for."

"You want her?" Walker didn't really need to ask the question but he felt obligated. The more Dex told him the more he wanted to go after her.

"I feel protective of her."

Walker nodded. He could read between the lines. Dex did have a thing for Cass, but not enough to pursue or push it. Which left him open to take her for himself. Now he just had to convince Cass she didn't need to run away.

"I'm going to see if I can find her. Make sure she's okay."

"Uh huh. She's probably gone. Cass isn't one for socializing around here. She has a need, gets it filled as best she can, and then goes back to her life to pretend everything will be fine.

"And where is that life?"

Dex shrugged. "No one knows, or at least no one says. There are people in the lifestyle who make it a point to know everything about everyone, but they also guard that information."

A pretty young girl arrived at the station, eager anticipation written on her face.

"Unfortunately, Walker, you're on your own with this one." With that his friend moved over to his next victim and led her to his cross.

Read More Now

ALSO BY E.M. GAYLE

CONTEMPORARY ROMANCE

Mafia Mayhem Duet Series:

MERCILESS SINNER

SINNER TAKES ALL

WICKED BEAST

WILLING BEAUTY

BROKEN SAINT

FALLEN ANGEL

Outlaw Justice Series:

SAVAGE PROTECTOR

RECKLESS PAWN

RUTHLESS REDEMPTION

Outlaw Justice: Sins of Wrath MC:

CRUEL SAVIOR

SCORCHED KING

VICIOUS DEFENDER

Purgatory Masters Series:

TUCKER'S FALL

LEVI'S ULTIMATUM

MASON'S RULE

GABE'S OBSESSION

GABE'S RECKONING

Purgatory Club:

ROPED

WATCH ME

TEASED

BURN

BOTTOMS UP

HOLD ME CLOSE

Pleasure Playground Series:

PLAY WITH ME

POWER PLAY

Single Title:

TAMING BEAUTY

WICKED CHRISTMAS EVE

BEARLY DATED

WOLF TEMPTED

Devils Point Wolves:

WILD

WICKED

WANTED

FERAL

FIERCE

FURY

Single titles:

REJECTED WOLF QUEEN

VAMPIRE AWAKENING

WITCH AND WERE

9 798215 803318